Death on The Rise

A Crime Novella

By John B. Manbeck

Published by John B. Manbeck

ISBN 13: 978-0692201916
ISBN 10: 0692201912

Produced by Digital Scanning Inc.

In this series:
The Disappearance of Patricia Murphey
Coming soon: *Skeleton in the Attic*

Also by John B. Manbeck:
Chronicles of Historic Brooklyn
Brooklyn: Historically Speaking
Historic Photos of Brooklyn
Historic Photos of The Brooklyn Bridge
The Brooklyn Film- with Robert Singer
The Neighborhoods of Brooklyn
Coney Island Kaleidoscope- with Lynn Butler

CREDITS:
Cover Layouts: Gail Smollon
Front Cover Photo *Credit:* John B. Manbeck

CHAPTER ONE

She paused on the sidewalk to adjust the seam in her hose, touch up her lipstick, make her beret a bit jauntier and push her chewing gum behind her ear. Then glancing at her tiny watch in disgust, she scanned the neighboring brownstones just as a cloud passed. She turned in to the only apartment building on the block, gray stone with leaded windows on the first two floors and small decorative balconies. On the frieze over the doors, miniature stone gargoyles stared down.

As she walked through the revolving door and over to the hotel desk, Nate Thomaston squinted at her, then up and down, hanging his thumbs under his suspenders and, on the left side, his shoulder holster. He checked the bobbed blonde hair, the crimson shade of lipstick and the tight skirt leaving a good bit of leg exposed. He smiled to himself and flicked a flame at the cigarette hanging from his lips.

She looked sideways at him and flashed a grin as she stepped away from the desk clerk and swung toward the elevator, watching the arrow above fall to Number 1. As the elevator door opened, she flipped her hip and glanced in his direction again. One of the advantages of being a house dick. Maybe, he thought, when she finishes....

1

Then her piercing scream cut through the morning quiet.

She had dropped her purse and pointed toward the floor of the elevator and screamed again before Nate could reach her and clamp his hand over her mouth. Then he stared into the dim interior, past the gate and involuntarily pulled her back, his fedora rolling down the hallway, sparks from his cigarette scattering to the carpet. "Jesus H. Christ!"

Twenty minutes later, Sgt. Dan Murphy from the Homicide Squad, his suit jacket flapping open and his belly parting the shirt buttons, stood in the lobby grilling the desk clerk. From outside, where two police runabout coupes had parked jaggedly at the curb next to a police Indian motorcycle, Lt. Jared Lewis pushed through the door, glared sourly at Thomaston and strode over to Murphy. The blonde, still pale but now snapping her rescued gum, wrenched herself from the policeman holding her arm, and almost fell onto the lieutenant. "Ya gotta believe me, mister. I ain't done nothin'. I just pushed the Up button and there he was."

He looked down at her. "And you were just here to visit your sick auntie, right?"

She nodded her head stepping aside for two ambulance attendants who pushed through carrying a bloodied stretcher covered by a stained white sheet. She grimaced.

"Well, there ain't no 'aunties' living in this building, dolly," interrupted Murphy, now at her elbow. "This is a gentlemen's hotel. Sure it's not your 'Mammy,' as Al Jolson would say? Maybe you had other things in mind? Maybe you even have some hooch stashed away back here?" He patted her rump. Nice. No girdle. "Now wait over there like a good little girl." She slung a curse at him and moved to a corner.

"What did the gumshoe have to say for himself?" asked Lewis, jerking his head toward Thomaston.

"Just that he never saw the corpus delecti before."

The lieutenant frowned, pushing up his cap. "You mean the stiff didn't live here?"

"Not only that. Thomaston never saw him come in."

"Some security he is. Did you find a weapon?"

"No. I mean, yes. It was a knife. But no, we didn't find it. Yet."

Lewis catalogued the newly painted lobby, its green walls and dark, beamed ceiling. He squinted out at the sunlit street, past the pillars where several uniformed officers chatted. Two street urchins in short pants gazed up at them, then over to the motorcycle. Must be from the Lower Hook, he surmised, not from The Heights.

"Let's both talk to Nate."

Nate rose from the leather chair behind the potted palm that had lost most of its leaves from the coffee diet Nate fed it. He shook his head in response to the lieutenant's question. "Nope. Never laid eyes on him. He was a tall one. Would've remembered him for sure."

Lewis studied him. "You're not holding out on us, are you?"

"Why should I, Lieutenant?" Nate sniffed.

"Just want to see if you smile and smile and are still a villain."

"Jesus!"

The lieutenant looked down the hallway, past where police questioned the few residents they could find. "How about other entrances, Nate? The basement?"

"Sure," Nate agreed. "We have one. But there's no way anyone could've gotten in that way. The gate to the alley is locked and so is the cellar door. With an alarm."

"Where's the super? Does he have keys?"

"You bet. But he ain't here today."

"Then where is he, wise guy?" demanded Murphy.

"Yeah. Where is he?" another voice interrupted.

"What the hell are you doing here, Jenkins?"

"Only my job. I'm a reporter, remember? A crime reporter."

"Oh, yeah. One of those foot soldiers that works for the *Eagle*. I heard of you guys." Murphy tilted his derby back. Then he turned back to Nate. "Where was we?"

"Where is he , you mean?" Jenkins added. "Where's the super? Right?"

Nate stretched. "Oh, probably in bed. With some broad. How the hell should I know?"

"Well," the lieutenant answered patiently while Murphy turned red, "let's see if we can get him over here, shall we, Mr. Thomaston? You know how the law works. You have an emergency number, don't you? 'For the want of a nail, a war was lost.' Right, Nate?" Lewis rocked back on his heels, his thumbs hooked on his Sam Browne belt.

"Sure." Nate pushed his fedora back. "I called him first thing. He's on his way. If he's not too drunk to find the place." Nate grinned at their discomfort.

"Some dump you have here." Murphy stuffed his pad back into his pocket. "Just keep your nose clean,

Thomaston. We'll talk later." Then he turned to his men questioning the tenants, lighting up a cigarette with his Zippo. "Don't let anybody go until me and the lieutenant sees them, OK? I want names and phone numbers of everyone in the building at the time. Well, what you looking at, boy?" he shot at the Negro porter, who jumped back at the accusation.

The investigation took the rest of the morning with fingerprint police spraying the elevator, handles and door knobs, plainclothesmen taking statements, and a lot of "Don't leave town." In spite of the warning, Nate slipped out the side door and ambled down to Court Street toward Joe's—for a cup of joe. With all those dumb coppers around, nobody would miss him.

Jenkins squeezed into the booth seat across from him. "Who invited you?" snapped Nate as he poured two mountainous spoonsful into the coffee cup and stirred.

"Just thought you needed company. You looked lonely."

"Not lonely for you, Jenkins. Scram, why don't ya? Skidoo, kiddo."

Jenkins just gazed at Nate. He was at least half Nate's age. With his shirtsleeves rolled up past his elbows and two pencils sticking out of his shirt pocket, he resembled more a school kid than a working man. His uncombed hair made him seem still younger but he was beginning to put on weight. Yet Nate heard he was a good writer with a following among the pols downtown. Not that he ever read that trash.

"Cuppa java with a bagel and schmooze on the side," Jenkins told the waiter. "OK, Nate, who's the bird? Was she a plant?"

"You're barking up the wrong tree, sonny. I never seen her before."

"Never? Or maybe never?"

"Never! Can't you understand?"

"Marty at the desk said she's been there before. Says you know her."

"He's a liar."

"Says you even know her name." The reporter rolled his pencil between his fingers, watching Nate's reaction. "Anyway, the cops got her at the cop shop. She'll squeal. She can't afford no time. You know that Cole Porter show that just opened on Broadway? It's got her theme song in it. Called 'Love for Sale.' Coincidence, no?"

"Look I said I don't know her. So lay off. Maybe it was my day off when she came by, OK? Say, Jenkins, I gotta make a phone call. You'll be gone when I get back. Right?" He grabbed a quick swallow from the cup and dashed for the red phone booth in the rear.

Damn him! Nate muttered as he pulled the booth door shut. He pretended to dial and talk into the mouthpiece until he saw Jenkins stand up, lift an abandoned newspaper from a near table and walk out chewing on his bagel. As soon as he was clear, Nate emerged, tossed a quarter on the table and headed for Foffe's around the corner on Montague, climbing to their door at the top of the stoop.

The restaurant had long been a hangout for politicians and police types. The air was so thick with cigarette and cigar smoke, it stung his eyes. Good customers could nurse

6

their drinks without comment. For specials, a bottle under the bar could suffice. At least, they were never raided since the dry days started. And talk on the circuit lay odds that the dry spell would soon be history. Nate squatted on a stool and nodded to Jake. A glass slid in front of him.

Studying the mirror over the bar, he watched Jimmy Donahue, the ward boss, work the room. The locals eased over to his table to drop a word or two in his ear, and then slink off. Jimmy sat at a table in the center of the room, alone with his steak, glass of real scotch and a big cigar, his napkin tucked into his shirt collar. Nate wished that he had some important information that Jimmy could use; that would make his day.

When the light faded outside and was switched on inside, Nate realized he'd stayed too long at the fair. He slapped several bills on the counter and carefully eased himself off the stool and down the stone steps, directing himself—again carefully—past Borough Hall and toward his single room in Vinegar Hill.

Long shadows loomed and danced as he moved from one street lamp arc to the next. Shapes in corners shifted. How it happened, he didn't remember. Was it the slippery cobblestones? Or did he trip on a bluestone lifted by the tree roots? Or was it a warning?

CHAPTER TWO

"Meet at the Automat or Bickford's?" Lewis said to the phone.

"For God's sake, the Automat," came the scratchy reply.

Lt. Lewis, now dressed in civilian clothes, searched the white marble room for Rosenthal. Then he spied him behind the cashier's booth. He poked a dollar under the glass, scooped up the nickels from the well and poured himself a coffee. "OK, Manny. I see you. Are you hiding out in plain sight? What gives?" He eased a dirty dish aside to make room for his cup.

"What? No cheese and macaroni today?" Rosenthal strained a smile but it had no effect on the lieutenant.

"Not for breakfast, wise guy."

"Saw the headlines this morning. Thought you'd like to know what I dug up." His face turned into a smirk.

Lewis pushed his hat back. "Let me guess." His deep blue eyes studied the lawyer's unshaved face. "Is it free?"

Rosenthal shrugged. "Someone will pay. I found paperwork that proves that certain numbers have been fudged."

"Who? What numbers?"

Rosenthal wagged a finger. "That would be telling tales out of school, Lieutenant. For a price, now, that's different."

"Sounds like you're withholding evidence to me. Maybe even blackmail."

"Now, now, Lieutenant, we're only talking hypothetical, right?" He unwrapped a stick of Black Jack gum and dropped the paper on the floor. "Let's just say maybe you have a revenge crime. Money's involved, really big bucks.Why? With bank business these days, everyone—and I mean everyone—is looking to find some slack. Now," he confided as he leaned closer, "if the wrong parties got burned, it could lead to some aggravation, if you get my gist. See? Now I got the payola dirt safely put away. Interested?"

"I get it. But I don't. What's in it for you?"

A grin oozed from Rosenthal's puffy lips. "Just a helping hand for my pal, Lieutenant. I might need a favor down the line."

"That's just what I thought." Lewis glared at him. "For Christ's sake, Manny, we don't even have a suspect yet."

"But I can get you one."

"No dice. You're rolling snake eyes, Manny. Once we get over that first hill, we need to win a conviction. Maybe the DA can use you then. I'll keep it in mind but to me you don't even get a base on balls. I don't know about you shysters." He stood up looming over Rosenthal's balding head. "Ever hear of Shylock? He was trying to collect on a bet. The defense lawyer argued that he could have his pound of flesh as long as he didn't shed a drop of blood." He smiled at Rosenthal's puzzled frown. "Try it some time, Manny. You're out for blood."

Back in the street, he merged into the crowd on the sidewalk.

9

"How's the investigation going, Murphy?" Lewis asked as he sank into his swivel chair with a sigh, absently leafing through new papers tossed onto his desk.

"Got a tenant on the top floor who claimed someone tried to get in his window from the fire escape last week. Name's Lenny Hamm." He turned to his pad. "Says he wants to be called Larry. Sissy kind of guy. A real Goofus. He's afraid of his own shadow. Worked in a back office. Got laid off I don't know when. Kinda feel sorry for him. Afraid of his shadow but his neighbors say he's an arithmetic whiz."

"Great. How long ago this break-in happen? A week ago, you say?" Lewis rubbed his long nose. "Was it a real break in?"

"Nope. The perp got scared off. That's why Hamm never reported it. Another one on the third floor thought he heard elevator noises early this morning. But he couldn't remember whether it was before or after the milkman came through the halls."

"How about the elevator operator? Anything there?"

Murphy shook his head. "Nope. Wasn't any. This is one of those newfangled automatic elevators. Self service. No operator."

"So what is it: an inside job or not?" Lewis picked up a pencil and started doodling on a pad.

Murphy shook his head. "Don't know yet. Just haven't got a lead. Still need an ID on the corpse." He sipped from a Dixie Cup on his desk. Then he checked his pad again. "The broad was pretty nervous, though. Said she'd talk to you if you could keep her off the books."

"Let's hear what she has to say. Bring her in. Say what's in that cup?"

CHAPTER THREE

Nate, still woozy, pulled himself upright from his bed, rubbing his head. Still dark and he hadn't even taken off his clothes. Splashing cold water on his face, he ran a comb through his hair and was down on Sands Street minutes later passing from pools of street lights to garish reflections from the dark bar windows. An old cap shadowed his eyes. He headed straight for a dive near the Navy Yard gates. Outside, a uniformed cop waited, smiled knowingly at him and then walked away down the sidewalk. So much for the law and Prohibition.

The smell of stale beer, cigarette smoke and sweat hit him before he stepped through the door. Gobs, both Navy and civilian, stood several deep at the bar, shouting their orders over the sounds from the juke box. While some tried feeling up the floozies, other women lifted bills from their pockets.

Nate worked his way to a corner where Mike, the bouncer, stood nursing a ginger ale. "Freddie's inside," Mike nodded toward a door.

"Understand some shit's headed your way," Freddie greeted him from behind an oversized mahogany desk.

"Yeah. I thought this was small time. Local stuff. Not murder."

"Can't help it, Nate. Every once in a while a few eggs get broken. Know what I mean?"

12

"Yeah, I hear you, but I don't like it. Someone may want to finish the job. How can I get them off my ass?" Nate raised his voice. "I need some space, Freddie."

Freddie shifted in his chair, a little man protected by a big desk. His pencil-thin mustache twitched. "Problem is our local guys are not the one's leaning on you. These guys could be from outa town."

"What do you mean 'could be'? You mean, you've never seen them before?"

"Yeah, it's a deal they worked up over in East New York. A contract. Sort of like a subscription service."

"Like *The Saturday Evening Post*?"

"Sort of. More like *The New York Post*. They call it Murder Inc. Know what I mean?"

Nate swallowed. "Not exactly. Talk."

"They work deals. Their guys fix our problems. We fix theirs. That way nobody knows who pulls the trigger. When the market crashed, the syndicate moved in to protect their investment. Know what I mean?"

Nate nodded, not at all happy. "Just tell them to lay off the rough stuff. Let me know what I have to do. OK?"

Freddie lifted a bottle and glass from his desk drawer. "If I can. If it's not too late. Take the alley out, Nate. Just don't trip over any of the girls."

Nate pushed the fire door open on to a side street where women stood under lights in varied stages of undress. Then he stopped.

She stepped out of the side room, a puzzled expression on her face. Her hair was tied in a French bun this time, not a bob, and her eyes mascaraed. Otherwise she was completely naked. A flawless, hairless body. Slim, curvy, alabaster white. In her hand, she held a smoking cigarette; on her feet were stiletto heels. She inhaled on the butt, blew a circle into the air and stepped back into the room, back into her own addled world.

Out of my league, thought Nate. But it's nice to see she has a real job.

CHAPTER FOUR

Murphy and the lieutenant hunched over scraps of paper at a long table, moving them around. "Before we question the lady, let's see what we have. OK, how many people live in the hotel?"

"Most are long term renters. A few rooms are kept on the ground and first floors for transients. But not the back rooms. About 73 total. Ten rooms on a floor. Ten floors plus a penthouse, which is empty. Not all the rooms are occupied. And not everyone was home. Some were at work. Some at the employment office. Some out of town."

"Interesting, Murphy. But just answer the question. How many…?"

"…were in the building? I'd say 28. But we were only able to question 19."

"Jeez. Only 19 out of 28? OK, let's work with that. Just start with residents whose windows open on the fire escape."

Murphy, his suspenders loose at his side, stepped over to the blackboard and ran some lines over it.

"Aside from Hamm on the top floor, we have Schultz on the second floor."

"Convenient. Any leads on him?"

"Not really. He thought he heard noises in the night but he don't hear too good. He's a cripple, too. Takes him a while to get around. No suspect there. Then Bates on 3. He says he was in the shower at the time. Lopez on 4 claimed he took a sleep draught and was dead to the world. On 5 we have a possibility. Jones."

"Why?"

"No alibi. Said he was home waiting. And he has a record. Had been a boxer. Says he's been straight since he served time."

"What was the charge?"

"Larceny. Not murder. Said he didn't hear nothing".

Lewis walked to the water cooler. "The rest?"

"Well, there's Gargulio on 6. Said he was on the subway but no one could vouch for him. He's an accountant. Donovan on 7. Don't really trust him. Shifty eyes. Even though he's a landsman. He works for a security firm."

"What's he look like?"

"Big. Just under 6 feet. Licensed to carry. Could be a possibility. But he said he had the grippe and he looks it. All worn out with sniffles. Cohen lives on 8. He moved in last week. Just got a job as a bank teller. Says he's thinking of moving out. Now."

"Can't blame him. On 9?"

"Stevenson. A kid who had to quit college in order to help his mom. Now works part time for a law firm. Also moved in recently."

"Anybody admit to renting the lady?"

"Not yet. She may not have been cheap but she wasn't expensive either. Used to be a taxi dancer before she got into the skin trade."

"OK. Let's hear what the two-bit whore has to say about her rendezvous."

When the lieutenant nodded, the matron at the door pushed her prisoner into the room, shaking her head in disgust.

"Sleep OK?" asked Murphy with a smirk.

"Ha!"

"Let's hear it. Who sent for you?"

She sat down, crossed her legs, smoothed her skirt and took out a cigarette pack. "Don't you guys ever take a bath?" she sniffed. She leaned over to straighten her hose.

"Don't give me that. And no smoking in the station house," Murphy reached for the Chesterfields. She quickly stuffed them back in her purse.

"OK, then, the basics. Name and occupation?"

She shrugged one shoulder. "I gave it to the desk sarge."

"Come on, Sadie."

"You hit the jackpot, Lieutenant. Sadie! That's it. Whoopee! You see that Eddie Cantor picture show? It's a good one with ol' banjo eyes."

The lieutenant stood up and straightened his uniform jacket. "We don't need this shit, Sadie. Have Hayes run a check on her for aliases. She thinks the whole goddam world's a stage. And she's the goddam star."

She sighed, trying to look coy and virginal.

"I thought you wanted to talk to me, bitch."

"Maybe I changed my mind."

Murphy, a lit cigarette in his mouth, leaned into her. "Again. What's your real name, Sadie?" He blew smoke at her.

"Get outa my face, buster." She squirmed away from his hand. "What's this, a quiz show? OK. The moniker's Sadie Blue."

"Damn it," growled Lewis. "your real name. Are you a loner or do you work out of the Behr house?"

"Hold on, Lieutenant. You already know I ain't killed nobody." Her gum cracked.

"Maybe we know that. Maybe we don't. Who were you visiting?"

"A party."

"Name? Room number?"

"They never give me no names. Room was 205."

Murphy glanced up from his scraps of papers. "We checked out 19 rooms. I don't think it was 205, Sadie."

"All 19? My, I can see why you're in charge of this case, Sergeant. I didn't think you had that many fingers."

"Just shut up and give me the right answers. Why did you need an elevator to go up to the second floor?"

"Maybe I was tired from working all night?"

"So far you've given us zilch." Lewis slapped his hand on the table. "Room 205 belongs to a war cripple who couldn't get it up for the likes of you. All lies. Charge her with mopery, Sergeant, and throw her in the hoosegow. Go cool your gams in a cell, Sadie." He signaled the matron to take her back. "Maybe she's some gangster's moll."

Sadie blanched. "Wait a minute, Lieutenant. You gotta believe me." She tried to pull away from the matron's grip. "I'd be mincemeat if I told you more."

"Yeah?" said Murphy. "You're mincemeat now, sister. Just don't tell us no more fairy tales." He hitched his pants up.

"OK. OK. It was 505." Then she giggled. "The prize fighter. He's been a regular. But don't let on I told you. OK?" She hid her mouth.

"Why"

"Just because."

The lieutenant nodded and reached for his cap. "Work on it, Dan. Keep her here until you get a straight answer. I gotta go and remind my wife I'm still alive."

Sadie giggled again.

Murphy nodded, still studying Sadie. "What's so funny?"

"Oh, one more thing, Murphy." The lieutenant turned at the door. "Check on when the tenants moved in. Tomorrow I'll give you a list of who I want to see."

CHAPTER FIVE

Nate met Jenkins in the makeup room of the *Eagle*. "This better be good, Jenkins. I had to get Wayne to cover for me," Nate yelled. Linotype machines clattered and the presses rumbled from below.

Jenkins smiled and led Nate to the framed layouts of tomorrow's paper. He took a pencil from behind his ear and pointed to a story locked in type and a photo plate on the metal table in front of him. "Look at this, Nate. I squeezed an interview out of Lewis. It'll run in the early edition."

"Now how in hell am I supposed to read that?" complained Nate. "It's all upside down and ass backward."

"Only backward," corrected Jenkins. "Come around this side and I'll read it to you."

Jenkins read from the page that the police had discovered a link between a resident of The Remsen Hotel and a *mafia* contact. Additional questioning and arrests were expected.

"Now who could that be?" Jenkins turned to Nate. "Who knows a little secret?"

"How the hell would I know?"

"Because your name was mentioned. But the coppers are waiting to close in on another suspect first. A lawyer."

"Rosenthal. That would be Manny Rosenthal."

"Oh, it all comes back to you now? Does he know anything?"

"I doubt it. He's just a tinhorn. Yeah, he's been a regular visitor. He knows a few people in the hotel. But he don't know nothing."

"According to a pigeon, he's gonna sing. Maybe it's a song called 'Brother, Can You Spare a Dime,' right? Now does that lady play your tune? Does she play your flute?"

"Not funny, Jenkins. I told you I don't know her."

Jenkins loosened his bowtie. "Didn't think it was funny. My girlfriend says I don't tell jokes very well. But my sources tell me otherwise. Now if you can't help me anymore, I just might not be able to help you later. When the time comes. And it's just around the corner." He hummed a tune.

"Fat chance!" But Nate's bravado was not as strong as earlier.

CHAPTER SIX

Nate walked out past the cashier's booth blinking at the bright sunlight. Good flick, he thought. That Wallace Beery is a tough actor. Nate did a little feinting step walking down the street, just as Beery had done in the movie.

He needed time to think and to be alone. Dark movie houses relaxed him. And that was the perfect movie to put him in the mood. All about a boxer on his way up—and down. Nate tried to piece the events together.

Was it two, three weeks ago he first saw the babe? Said she had an interview with Mr. Jones on 5. Came over from the city. Damn! Brooklyn streets are really screwed up, she complained. Jones needed a secretary, she said. What does a boxer need a secretary for? Not one dressed in a sheath dress like that, accentuating all her curves. Trying to look like a lady with that cute flowered hat, white gloves and swinging that little handbag. OK, he told the desk clerk, I'll take her up.

Once the elevator doors closed, she turned toward him, rubbing her hips against him. So he copped a feel and she didn't complain. Now he knew. But what was the angle with Jones? He waited on 5 for the room door to open. She slipped in to the room and he returned to the lobby.

The next time he had a day off he visited the library where he found a copy of *Sporting News*. Nothing there. But the librarian told him about the *Police Gazette*.

"Richard Fox, the late publisher, was big on boxing," she explained as she leafed through a catalog. "But we don't subscribe to those kinds of magazines." Her smile made Nate think she wished otherwise.

It took a couple of tries but he found a Hotaling's News Store that had a copy. He called the number inside the publication's page and was told by the receptionist that the *Police Gazette* had articles on two Joneses. But one was an obituary on a fighter during the turn of the century.

"You can buy a back copy from our Circulation Desk, sir. But it's closed now."

It was another week before he got over to The City to buy a copy. But, boy, was it worth it! Talk about *The Champ.*

CHAPTER SEVEN

"OK, Murphy. What's new this morning?"

While the sergeant wore the same suit, Lewis had a gray double breasted three-piece on instead of his uniform. He took off his jacket and unbuttoned his vest, shifting his holster under his arm. His blue eyes seemed to almost twinkle.

"You're looking better, Lieutenant. A good meal must have helped."

"Forget the malarkey. What's new?"

"Wish I could get some decent grub but my brother, he don't cook so good. The old lady, now she knew how to cook an egg. You gotta hold on to them if you want to get fed."

"You don't look starving."

"OK. OK." Murphy flipped through his notes. "We found the weapon at the bottom of the trash chute. A hunting knife. Wiped clean. Got samples of the blood from the elevator carpet. Sent it to the lab." He closed his notebook. "Any record on the stiff?"

"Not yet," answered Lewis. "Not in our files, anyway. Must be from out of town. Who did you question so far?"

"Donovan I saw this morning. He started spouting off who he thinks is suspicious. Just what we need. A Sherlock Holmes. He said the mob's behind it. Could be. But I think he's clean. I'll talk to Cohen after three when the bank closes. Damn!" He reached down to remove his shoe. "That stone has been killing me," he complained as he shook it to the floor. "And Gargulio this evening. I'll see him then. That Gargulio. There's something about him that bugs me."

"Just like that stone? Did you send for Mr. Jones?"

"Tracey's bringing him in. Did you see that guy? He's something else." He lit a cigarette, blowing the smoke away. "Oh, the lab report. The lab reported the only blood samples were in the elevator, not in the hall. Or in any of the rooms. So he never left the elevator."

"Let's hear what Jones has to say. No alibi for yesterday, you said?" He hooked a pair of wire glasses over his ears to read reports on his desk.

"Jones said he was reading the 'Help Wanted' ads and waiting. You know, you read too many books, Lieutenant. Look at you. Younger than me and already you need reading glasses. That Shakespeare must have gotten to your brain. Bet you own Modern Library's complete set of Shakespeare."

"Drop it, Murphy. Let's just get this case out of the way before the captain gets antsy and Commissioner Whalen gets wind of it. Casey has another case for me to work on. A suicide from one of the uppity families. Sounds like a barrel of laughs."

"Step over to that desk," said a new voice. The plainclothesman moved from behind his prisoner, and all three men gazed up at the new man's face. Then at the cap in his hands. Then at his hands. Jones wore overalls and workman's boots. Lewis couldn't help thinking of the prisoner in Dickens' *Great Expectations.*

"Have a seat, Mr. Jones."

Jones nodded. Sitting down, he was the same height as the men in the room. "Name? Occupation?" asked Murphy.

"Am I under arrest, officer?" Jones had a high pitched voice that contradicted his size.

"No. We just want to ask some questions. Full name?"

Jones squirmed. "Rod Jones."

"Is that your full name? Is Rod your Christian name?"

Jones scowled. "I ain't no Christian. My name is Ethelrod." His face colored as he gazed at the floor. "And I ain't done nothing. Except for that girl."

"What did you do to the girl?"

"Just waited."

Lewis and Murphy turned to each other.

"Know anybody else in the building?"

"No. Just the girl. Oh. I met Larry once."

"OK. That's the guy on the top floor? So what were you doing before the murder? Before 10 o'clock?"

"Nothing. Just waiting for the girl. But she was late."

"Late?" questioned the lieutenant.

Jones just nodded, still staring at the carpet. "Yeah, late. She never should have been late. I never left my room until a cop knocked on my door. I was still waiting for the girl. She was late."

CHAPTER EIGHT

The lieutenant rode up front, leaning over the back of his seat to talk with Murphy while the police driver ran the lights, his siren on. Lewis sat with his cap on his knees, almost pushing the dashboard.

"Two days ago, Manny wanted to sell me information," he explained. "Told him I wasn't buying. But he was just a tease. Never named names. Now that Gargulio spilled the beans about what he overheard, maybe Manny can fill in the blanks."

"I don't think he's involved but we can use him as a material witness." Murphy leaned forward, holding the side strap. "It might be enough to turn the state's evidence. Telling that reporter might have been too soon, though."

"Don't think so. Maybe the *mafia* will get itchy when they read it," Lewis reasoned. "I didn't tell Jenkins what we found from Gargulio about the connection with insider trading. Since the crash, everyone's been suspicious of banks and investments. We should have seen that angle. Besides, the paper won't hit the streets for several hours. By then we'll have Manny safe in a cell."

The police car swerved past a traffic tower and between a trolley car and homeward bound cars, the driver downshifting and sending pedestrians dashing for the safety zone. "Where does this creep live?" asked the sergeant.

"Here in Flatbush. He's almost my neighbor. It's called Ditmas Park."

27

The Packard sedan turned into a residential street with large, gothic styled houses boasting wooden stairs, porches and colorful front lawns. The driver turned off the siren and rolled to the curb. Lewis and Murphy peeled out of the car, their hands on their weapons.

A Negro maid answered their ring. From a back room the Ipana Troubadours sang "Body and Soul" from a radio.

"Who should I say is calling?" she asked as the police edged into the vestibule.

"Friends. The police."

As she slid the pocket doors open, they followed her to a study in the back but no one answered her knock. She gently opened the door and then screamed.

"Too late," observed the lieutenant as he contemplated Manny's body on the floor, and then his eyes shifted to the shattered window opening on a rear garden.

"And where were you?" the sergeant turned to the shivering maid braced against the wall.

"I don't know, sir. When Mr. Rosenthal came home, he went straight to his office and closed the door. I told him I had to go around the corner for some greens and I'd be right back. He just nodded. And that's the last I saw of him. Till now."

The lieutenant was on the house phone calling emergency. "And send the black maria."

The maid gaped at him, terrified.

"Not for you," he explained. "For your boss. Anyone else in the house?"

She shook her head. "Then we'll just need a statement from you. After that you can get your things and go."

"Well," said the sergeant, "there goes our witness." He glanced at the papers strewn over the floor. "Guess our evidence is gone too. Let's go back to square one."

CHAPTER NINE

After his shift, Nate trudged down the street, his hands in his pockets, thinking about the note Charlie had sent him, almost bumping into a young couple. Only when he passed them did he realize it was Jenkins gazing at a pretty young woman on his arm. And he was all dressed up: a jacket, different bow tie, hair combed, shoes shined. The girl was a looker, too. Trim with nice long legs that went all the way up. Good taste for a newspaper slob.

From the corner, he watched them enter the doors of The Bossert. Then he realized it was Saturday night, dance night on the roof garden. He could even hear the music wafting gently through the evening air. Guess they were broadcasting, too. About to cross Montague Street, Nate suddenly remembered a question he wanted to ask Jenkins. Abruptly, he turned just as a Buick touring car swept around the trolley car, and past him through the Full Stop sign. He shot a glance at the covered license plate and realized that was not accidental. Thoughts of Jenkins vanished from his mind.

When the operator opened the elevator doors at the roof, Jenkins guided his date by the elbow as they followed the maître d' to a table by the broadcast booth. The girl, open-mouthed, gazed at the view, a panorama of the Manhattan skyline. "This is the Waldorf Astoria of Brooklyn," he whispered in her ear. He ordered drinks and glanced at the menu.

As the band swung into a lively Lindy hop, Jenkins and his partner eased onto the floor and then dived and swung out in rhythm to the drummer's rim shots and the wail of the tenor man.

After a slow number, he walked her back to their drinks, whispered to her again and stepped over to the radio control room. Jenkins asked a question of the announcer who pointed to the news teletype machine in a corner booth. The reporter read the message coming in over the wire, then turned to other stories hanging on a nail.

He smiled. Detroit.

On the way back to the table, his shoulders relaxed more and his broad smile greeted the young woman. Standing, she kissed him softly before they blended into the other couples on the dance floor. The lead trumpet stood for a sweeping solo on "Memories of You," driving the dancers deeper into each other's arms. Jenkins gave the girl a squeeze.

CHAPTER TEN

Freddie explained it to Nate. "No way, Nate. Know what I mean? These guys don't like losing. And you ain't got enough to pay them back. Know what I mean?"

"But if I could just talk to them—or him."

"No way. No excuses. They just don't take excuses. You were supposed to be the lookout, as I understand. And you weren't looking. So now you're out. Know what I mean? No second chances. Just stay out of their way. If you can. Know what I mean?"

"Yeah. I know. And you know how to contact me?"

"At the morgue? I'll see what I can do."

When Nate got back to the hotel, Marty signaled him to the desk. "A note for you. From the coppers."

Damn, he thought, as he read the note. As if I don't have enough troubles. "Marty, do you have Wayne's number? I gotta get him to sub for me once more. And it's gonna cost me. They want me down at the Poplar Street station. I don't know how long it's gonna take. I can't have you cover for me again today."

"OK, Nate. I'll give him a ring. Leave it to me." Marty, smiled, always willing to help Nate. And all the roomers, too, long term or overnight.

"Thanks, kid."

The desk sergeant at the precinct directed Nate to a room in the back. A uniformed cop at the door opened it for him. Except he wasn't wearing his full uniform, only in shirt sleeves with his tie loosened. Inside, Murphy and

Lewis, also in their shirtsleeves, indicated a chair. No smiles.

"Hot here," started the lieutenant, waving his hand toward a fan. "Take off your jacket, if you'll be more comfortable."

"How long am I gonna be here? I'm still on duty."

"Depends on you."

"We've been talking to Grace…." Murphy referred to his pad as Nate worked his tie loose.

"Grace? I don't know no Grace," shot back Nate.

"Maybe you know her as Sadie."

"Oh."

"Grace is her real name. Grace Eldridge. From Detroit."

"So?"

"So she spilled some beans, wise guy. You know you keep on this way, we can have your gun permit lifted." Lewis turned to Murphy. The sergeant continued in a quieter tone. "OK. Sadie said you both knew the stiff in the elevator. True?"

"I got nothing to say."

"From Detroit? That ring any bells? Willie? Harry? Tony?"

"Good God!"

"That rattle your little pea brain, Nate? Because that policeman outside the door is a stenographer and he can take it all down."

"OK. But I need some protection."

"We'll see what we can do," offered the lieutenant as he opened the door. "Maybe you want a mouthpiece, too?"

As the man put his pad on the table, another uniformed man rushed into the room. "A radio call for you, Lieutenant. Urgent." He thrust a note at him.

"Christ! Come on, Murphy, more leg work." He slipped on his jacket and grabbed his cap from the rack. "You, too, Thomaston. This involves you. Probably more than you wish."

CHAPTER ELEVEN

As the patrol car squealed to a stop in front of the hotel, Nate surveyed the crowd of neighbors, residents and onlookers gathered behind the wooden horses in front of the building. Glittering shards of glass spread over the sidewalk. The hotel doors stood strangely open. Attendants from the two ambulances busily dashed between stretchers on the ground. A uniformed sergeant walked over to the lieutenant.

"A drive-by shooting. Tommy guns. Nobody got the license but we got a description: black Buick sedan, this year's model."

"Great," said Lewis. "How many possibilities can that fit? Who are they treating?" He nodded toward the attendants.

"The house dick, the desk clerk and the porter. The dick and the boy got dead. The clerk got lucky."

Lewis swung toward Nate. "Looks like you're the real lucky one, Nate. Maybe you'll last long enough to reach the next age of Man."

Nate just blinked and fired up a cigarette, inhaling deeply. "OK. So what do you want to know?"

"Everything. From Gargulio we know that Jones on 5 and Hamm on 10 have a relationship. They both moved in on the same day. Right?"

Nate nodded.

"Anything else?"

"Jones was a bodyguard for the little guy. Hamm was a financial genius. He knew how to fix books. And he did it for some local hoods. But he picked the wrong account."

"And?"

"He was supposed to be roughed up by these out of town mobsters. Just to throw a little scare into him, they said."

"And you were the lookout. Right?"

Nate nodded. "But what I don't get, he said, is why little Marty had to get it?"

"That's just the way the cards fall, Nate," answered Murphy. "It should have been you."

Lewis walked over to the ambulance attendant as he climbed in. The other ambulance waited for the morgue wagon.

"They think he's going to make it," Lewis reported back. "Now we want to wrap this up. See the *Eagle* story by Lars Jenkins? He reported about an infiltration of gangsters from Detroit." Drawing a copy of the paper from his jacket, he put on his glasses to check and then handed it over to Nate. "As if we don't have enough of the home grown brand. Now here's what we want you to do."

CHAPTER TWELVE

Nate strapped his revolver tight and pulled his cap lower to shade his eyes. Being blinded by a light is the last thing he wanted to happen. The quiet of daytime Sands Street seemed eerie.

Amazingly, Freddie had contacted him again and said the guys wanted to see him. For what? Is it a trap? They gonna take me for a ride? Nate had asked.

"Not from my place. I'll have my boys around and they know it. Beyond my doors, I can't say. Know what I mean?"

Nate wasn't sure anymore.

Of course they searched him as soon as he entered the bar. And took away his shoulder gun.

No cop on the beat this early. The sun shone brightly through the skylight. Nate thought the sun could never penetrate that smoke and grime.

Escorted to Freddie's office, he saw a stranger behind Freddie's desk. No greeting. No rough stuff. Just "Let's take a ride, mister. We'll talk."

So that's it.

On the way out the side door, the stranger struck up a friendly conversation. "Thought you'd like to know that your girlfriend's no longer among us," he grinned.

Nate hadn't expected that. He tensed. The driver jerked his chin toward the street. "Look." An man in a wheelchair began crossing in front of the Buick.

"Run him over."

The driver revved the motor as the other Detroit boys reached for the doors. One crumbled over the running board, a bullet through his head. The wheelchair toppled, its occupant firing from behind it.

When the raid started, Nate fell to the ground, reaching for his ankle holster. He got one shot off at the driver. "That's for Sadie," he muttered before he felt a burning pain in his arm. Rolling under the car, he watched as a fusillade of bullets from a battery of cars at the end of the alley took down another one and shattered the car's lights. A third fell running down the street.

After the visitors lost another, they surrendered, outnumbered and outgunned. The home team won, seeing as the FBI had backed them up. If only the Dodgers could synchronize their plays as well as this team.

After his release from Long Island Hospital, Nate walked over to the hotel with his arm in a sling. Workmen had replaced the glass in the front doors and the chinks in the cement. Marty, on crutches, leaned on the desk.

After the lobby is fixed up, he explained, the hotel will be sold. "Hotels can't stand that kind of bad publicity. So the owners decided to operate as a rental building. They offered me the job as the super. Maybe when the market picks up, they'll make other plans."

Nate worked his way through the shopping crowds on Montague Street down to the precinct house. There he surrendered his license and his gun and left the property office with a receipt in his hand.

As he turned, a hand clasped his shoulder. "Take some weight off your feet, Nate. Just caught me on my way out," Murphy moved to the time clock. "Me and my brother are driving back to Philly to check out the old homestead. Lost my mom last month and we have to settle things."

"Sorry to hear that." Nate shrugged his shoulders. "So what else did you figure out?"

The policeman laughed. "Some nutty case, Nate. Hamm had cooked the books and his bosses found out. So they gave him the boot even though he was a genius at his brokerage house but not too smart elsewhere. They just didn't want to put up with the nuisance and the trouble.

"Hamm got terrified, really shaking in his boots. The pressure was on. So he got a bodyguard: Jones. Think your buddy Freddie made the contact. But they had to have rooms on separate floors so no one would get suspicious. Meanwhile, that morning Jones was waiting for this broad, right? She was supposed to be a decoy to leave it clear for the Detroit hood.

"Hey, Jimmie," he called. "Get me a Coke from the ice box, OK? Make it a deuce." Murphy popped the cap with a church key from his pocket.

"But Jones got restless just waiting for the broad and decided to go up and visit Hamm. That would show her, he thought, if he wasn't there. It served her right. Meanwhile, the Detroit man had taken the fire escape to the second floor. He knew, from you, that the cripple there was restricted to his bedroom and had hearing problems, too. So the goon goes through the apartment, gets the elevator up to 10. Now on 5, Jones gets in the elevator, much to Detroit's surprise. But Jones is not as dim as he seems to be. So when Detroit takes a blade to Jones, he sees it as a threat. Well, you know Jones' size. He didn't have much trouble disarming Detroit but then the jerk goes after him again.

That's when Jones sliced him to pieces. Self defense, we figure. Then Jones takes the stairs back to his apartment to wait for Sadie. Hamm didn't even know how close he came. But he's the one that may be in deep doodoo now."

"Gonna run him in?"

"Yep. Hey, where are my manners? Here's your poison." Murphy handed the second bottle to Nate.

"So that's it?"

"It got a little more complicated. We rode up to question Hamm. His door was open and there he was, sprawled on the floor."

"Dead?"

"No. But almost. The Detroit gang had delivered their message and roughed him up a bit. A black eye and a broken nose. Some kicks in the ribs. But he'll live to face trial."

"So," Murphy looked up from his bottle, "me and the lieutenant wants to know what you're going to do, knowing that the hotel is converting and all that. He's over at H&H pigging out on mac and cheese."

Nate took a sip. "I decided to go to Easy Street and get in another line of work. It's in the same field. Except it's not." He stopped for dramatic effect. "I thought I'd sell insurance."

www.ingramcontent.com/pod-product-compliance
Lightning Source LLC
Chambersburg PA
CBHW070652130626

46555CB00006B/2841